Foul Ball Frame-up at Wrigley Field

The Baseball Geeks Adventures Book 2

THE BASEBALL GEEKS ADVENTURES

Foul Ball Frame-up at Wrigley Field

The Baseball Geeks Adventures Book 2

David Aretha

Speeding Star

Wrigley Field™ is a registered trademark and is owned by the Chicago National League Ball Club, L.L.C. This story has not been authorized by Wrigley Field™ or the Chicago National League Ball Club, L.L.C.

Library of Congress Cataloging-in-Publication Data

Aretha, David.
  Foul ball frame-up at Wrigley Field / David Aretha.
    pages cm. — (The Baseball Geeks adventures ; book 2)
  Summary: When eleven-year-old Omar is unfairly blamed by the media for a Chicago Cubs loss at home, his fellow Baseball Geeks try to clear his name.
  ISBN 978-1-62285-123-2
  1. Wrigley Field (Chicago, Ill.)—Juvenile fiction. 2. Chicago Cubs (Baseball team)—Juvenile fiction. [1. Wrigley Field (Chicago, Ill.)—Fiction. 2. Chicago Cubs (Baseball team)—Fiction. 3. Baseball—Fiction. 4. Blame—Fiction.] I. Title.
  PZ7.A6845Fo 2014
  [Fic]—dc23   2012049039

Future editions:
Paperback ISBN: 978-1-62285-124-9   EPUB ISBN: 978-1-62285-126-3
Single-User PDF ISBN: 978-1-62285-127-0   Multi-User PDF ISBN: 978-1-62285-168-3

To Our Readers: This is a work of fiction. References in this story are made concerning historical and current baseball players, otherwise any resemblance to actual persons, living or dead, is purely coincidental.

Speeding Star
Box 398, 40 Industrial Road
Berkeley Heights, NJ 07922
USA
www.speedingstar.com

Cover Illustration: © Ingvard the Terrible

CONTENTS

Chapter 1

ROLLING INTO CHICAGO

After nine antsy hours in Mr. Ovozi's Pontiac Aztek, we finally reached our destination city.

"Welcome to Chicago" stated the green sign, which glistened in the September sun.

"We made it, dudes!" exclaimed Kevin, our anxious friend, who high-fived Omar and me in the backseat. "The City of Big Shoulders."

"The City That Works," added Omar, our African-Uzbek-American pal.

"Who said 'City That Works'?" boomed Mr. Ovozi through his accent.

"That's what they call Chicago," replied Omar.

"So what, Chicago is the only city that works?" Mr. Ovozi said. "At my company, we bust our humps six days a week. Come to Cleveland—I'll show you a city that works."

Mr. Ovozi took the weekend off to take us Clevelanders to Chicago. His brother, who lives there, had four extra Cubs tickets. That evening, we were going to Wrigley Field™! And what a game: the first-place Cubbies vs. the second-place Cincinnati Reds—under the lights.

For Omar, Kevin, and me—known in our school as the Baseball Geeks— this would be the first big-league game we ever attended outside of Cleveland.

Of course, some still wonder if the Cleveland Indians *are* a big-league team.

"So who has the more pathetic history?" I asked. "The Cubs or the Indians?"

"Pathetic or cursed, Joe?" asked Kevin.

"Cursed," Omar said.

That was a good question. The Cubs hadn't won the World Series since 1908—or even been there since 1945. Some Chicagoans blame the "Curse of the Billy Goat." During that '45 season, Billy Sianis attended a World Series game at Wrigley Field. Sianis, who owned the Billy Goat Tavern, brought his pet goat to the game. That sounds cute, but the old goat stank, which bothered fans. Wrigley officials asked Sianis to leave and take his smelly goat with him.

On his way out, an angry Sianis declared, "Them Cubs, they aren't gonna win no more." And they didn't.

"And that's the Curse of the Billy Goat," I said.

"Yeah," said Omar, as he straightened his Indians cap. "But we have the 'Curse of Bobby Bragan.'"

The Indians last won a World Series in 1948. Four years after that, they fired manager Bragan. According to legend, Bragan returned to Cleveland Municipal Stadium and placed a curse on the team.

Ever since, the Indians have been plagued by bad luck. Just one example: In spring 1987, the Indians made the cover of *Sports Illustrated*. The headline read: "Believe it! Cleveland is the best team in the American League!" They finished the season with a record of 61–101.

"But the Indians were good in the '90s," I said.

"Yeah," said Omar, "but they never went all the way."

That's right. They were on the verge of making the playoffs in 1994, but then the major-league players went on strike and the playoffs were canceled.

In 1997, they were leading Game 7 of the World Series 2–1 in the ninth. But the Florida Marlins came back to win.

"Still," Kevin said, "that's nothing compared to the black cat."

Kev was referring to another Cubs curse. On September 9, 1969, the Cubbies were in first place in the National League East, ahead of the second-place New York Mets. But that day at the Mets' Shea Stadium, a black cat ran onto the field while the Cubs were batting.

A black cat is a symbol of bad luck, and the Cubs fell victim. They lost that game and fell into a bad slump. The Mets went on to win the World Series.

Through heavy traffic, Mr. Ovozi inched his way down Clark Street in Wrigleyville. I'd never seen a street as cool as this. Lining both sides were restaurants, pubs, theaters, and shops. We passed Murphy's Bleachers, Nuts on Clark, The Cubby Bear lounge. The streets were swarming with people, many of whom were in Cubs clothes.

"Let's not forget the ugliest hex of all time," Kevin said. "The Bartman Curse."

Poor Steve Bartman. He was just a regular guy, in a Cubs cap and glasses, rooting his team to victory.

"But he was in the wrong place at the wrong time," Omar said.

It was Game 6 of the 2003 National League Championship Series. The Cubs led three games to two over Florida. They were leading this game 3–0 in the eighth inning, with one out. All they needed was five more outs to reach the World Series for the first time in fifty-eight years.

That's when the Marlins' Luis Castillo lofted a fly ball to left field. It was a foul ball near the stands, but Cubs left fielder Moises Alou felt he could catch it. He arrived at the wall and reached over to make the grab. But at the same moment, Bartman—who was sitting in the front row—tried to catch it, too. He got his hands on the ball, preventing Alou from making the catch.

Bartman hadn't realized that Alou was below him. He had been concentrating on the ball in the sky. He felt terrible for his mistake. Fans started yelling and throwing things at Bartman, and security guards escorted him out of the park.

The Marlins scored eight runs that inning and won the game 8–3. They then beat the Cubs the next day to win the series. The whole episode ruined the poor guy's life.

Prior to that game, Bartman had been a Little League coach whom all the kids liked. After the game, he was getting death threats.

People hated him—just because he had reached for a baseball. He had to go into hiding, and reporters staked out his house.

"Bartman didn't do anything wrong," Omar said.

"Yeah," Kevin said, "but if he had been in the men's room that inning, the Cubs would have gone to the World Series."

"All I can say," Omar concluded, "is I'm glad I wasn't in his shoes."

As we drove further down Clark Street, Mr. Ovozi's face lit up.

"Look at this, guys!"

Peering out the window of the Aztek, we saw it: the world-famous red sign, towering above us. "Wrigley Field: Home of Chicago Cubs," it said.

"Whoa . . . ," Kevin said, wide-eyed.

"Awesome," Omar added.

After Mr. Ovozi paid for parking ("Forty dollars!" he exclaimed), we finally got out of that darn car. Omar stretched his long arms and wiggled his fingers. Kevin, who's kinda short, like me, marveled at the statues outside the old park. His favorite was the one of Hall of Fame shortstop Ernie Banks. "Mr. Cub" always had a smile on his face. He's the guy who said, "It's a great day for baseball. Let's play two!"

The atmosphere outside the ballpark was electric. The Cubs were six games ahead of the Reds in the standings with just eleven games to go. Fans could "taste" the playoffs.

A group of young women in Cubs T-shirts clapped their hands and chanted "LET'S go, CUB-bies!" A trio of jazz musicians played "Sweet Home Chicago" on their horns.

The smell of hot dogs was in the air, and the noise of the gathering crowd grew louder and louder. My body tingled as we waited in line with our tickets.

But today, as I look back on that September evening, I'm haunted by our discussion of Steve Bartman. "I'm glad I wasn't in his shoes," Omar had said.

Little did he realize that in less than three hours, he would be.

Chapter 2

THE CURSE OF OMAR

~~~~~~~~~~~~~~

"Hey, hot dog here!" boomed the chubby Wrigley vendor. "Who needs one?"

"I do," Kevin said, raising a $5 bill.

"You got it, pal," the vendor replied.

It was the fifth inning, and Kevin and I were sitting in the left-field seats. We were in the lower level, in foul territory, a couple rows behind the Ovozis. Omar and his dad sat in our section but in the first row.

The place was packed. Loud chatter was constant, and between-innings organ music added to the ballpark ambience.

The vendor yanked a boiled weenie and a moist bun out of his containers.

"What do you want *on* it, slugger?" he asked.

"Just ketchup," Kev said.

"Ketchup?" the vendor retorted. "You must be an out-of-towner, 'cause Chicagoans don't put ketchup on their dogs."

"We're actually from Cleveland," Kevin said.

"Oh, yeah?" the vendor replied with a chuckle. "Indians fans?"

We nodded.

"You have my sympathies," he said. "I predict a Cubs–Indians World Series— in the year 5000."

We smiled, and Kev paid the guy five bucks for a $4.50 dog.

"Keep the change," Kevin said.

"Thanks, champ," the guy said. "Go Tribe. . . . Hot dog here! . . ."

"That guy's like one of those 'Chee-ca-go' guys," Kevin said.

"Yeah," I said. "I thought he was gonna start saying, 'Da Bears! Da Bulls!'"

Kev with a Chicago accent: "Yeah, after all dose beef sanwiches, I dink I'm gonna have anudder hart attack!"

We cracked up.

Wrigley Field was a whole lot of fun. There's no other ballpark like it. The outfield fence is made of red brick, and that brick is completely covered with ivy (green vines and leaves). The park is a hundred years old, and a large, green manual scoreboard towers in center field.

Wrigley is the only major-league park that sits in a neighborhood. People live in condo buildings across the streets. You can see a bunch of the buildings behind the outfield bleachers. In fact, some people have constructed bleachers on top of the condo buildings. They watch the games from their rooftops!

"This place is awesome," Kevin said through a bite of his hot dog.

Kevin was a different person at Wrigley. He was normally a nervous Nellie, but Wrigley had a way of putting fans in a good mood.

Except the two guys directly behind us. They were about nineteen or twenty years old—and obnoxious. One guy wore a Reds cap; the other a Joey Votto Reds jersey. Both were big muscular guys—like football players—with neatly shaved heads. They continuously heckled the Cubs, who were leading 4–2.

"NINE-teen, OH-eight!" they chanted, referring to the year the Cubs last won the World Series. "It's choking time, Castro!"

"I heard Babe Ruth called this place a dump," said the guy in the cap.

"It smells like one," said the other. "And the hot dogs taste like the crap they serve in our cafeteria."

Kevin rolled his eyes. It was hard for us to ignore them.

Down below, I saw Omar eating something out of a cardboard basket.

"What do you think the Big O is eating?" I asked Kevin.

"Oh, I saw those," he said. "Cholula Tater Tots. They're potatoes with sour cream, cheese, and hot sauce."

"The hot sauce is probably why he needs that giant Pepsi," I said.

Omar appeared to be enjoying himself. He was pointing to the field and explaining a lot to his dad. Like, "On a fly ball, the runner on third has to go back and tag the base."

Mr. Ovozi is from Uzbekistan, and I'm sure they don't know much about baseball in that Eastern European country.

Thankfully, we no longer had to deal with the Reds fans. After Cincinnati couldn't score in the sixth, they left in a huff.

"Cubs suck!" one of them yelled as they walked away.

"What sucks," Kevin said to me, "is mean people. Let's hope we never become jerks like those guys."

"I hear ya," I said.

Soon we all rose for the Seventh Inning Stretch. At Wrigley, broadcaster Harry Caray used to lean out of his WGN booth and sing "Take Me Out to the Ball Game" with the fans. Ever since he died in 1998, celebrity guests have entered the booth and sung the song—from race-car driver Jeff Gordon to singer Ozzy Osbourne. On this day, a player on the Chicago Bears led the rendition.

In front of us, Omar and his dad sang along and swayed to the song. Omar turned and gave Kev and I a thumbs-up and a beaming smile.

But twenty minutes later, everything went horribly wrong.

In the top of the ninth, the Cubs led 4–2, but the Reds were threatening. With two outs, Cincinnati had runners on first and second. That's when the newest Cubs curse began—and our friend Omar was right in the middle of it.

A Reds slugger lofted a high fly ball to down the left-field line. Andres Cabrera—the Cubs' superstar left fielder—raced into foul territory near the wall. With the ball headed in our general direction, I took a quick picture with my cell phone camera.

Fans in the first three rows crowded together—right around Omar—trying to catch the foul ball. I couldn't see what happened, but most everyone else in the ballpark could. The fans' reaction can only be described as a collective gasp, followed by a large "Ohhhhh."

"What's going on?" I asked Kevin.

"Look," he said.

The woman in front of us was watching the game live on her iPad. We leaned over and saw Cabrera screaming at the third base umpire. The fans were booing their lungs out.

"Why's Cabrera all wet?" I asked.

"Somebody spilled their pop on him," the woman said.

They showed the replay: as Cabrera was waiting to make the catch, a fan in the first row—several feet above Cabrera—dropped his large Pepsi on the player's head! Temporarily blinded by the beverage, Cabrera couldn't catch the ball. It fell harmlessly foul.

Now we watched the "action" on the field. Cabrera was enraged with the umpire, claiming that the ump should have ruled "fan interference." Cabrera thought the ump should have called the batter out, which would have ended the game.

Cubs manager Joe Hargrove tried to corral his star player, but Cabrera broke free and shoved the ump. In baseball, that's a huge no-no.

"Oh, he's so gonna get suspended," Kevin said.

The umpire ejected Cabrera from the game, eliciting a huge "boooo" from the crowd. While that was happening, a ruckus brewed in the first few rows. Fans were throwing cups and paper wads and food at, of all people, Omar!

"Loser!" someone cried.

"Go home, you moron!" shouted another.

I looked at Kevin, and he at me.

"That was *his* Pepsi!" I said.

We looked at the replay on the iPad. The fans were bunched together, so it was hard to tell exactly what was going on. But sure enough, the large cup of Pepsi fell out of Omar's hand.

"Oh, my gosh," Kevin said.

Amid the bedlam, security guards were surrounding Omar and his father, shielding them from flying objects. They escorted the Ovozis toward the exit.

"Kick 'em out!" a fan yelled.

Since the Ovozis were our ride, we had no choice but to follow. Kevin's vacation from his anxieties was over. Stress lines returned to his face.

"Where are they taking him?" Kev asked.

I had no clue. But we followed the Ovozis as the guards rushed them out of the seating area and down the concourse—the walking area between the seats and the food stands.

"Omar!" I yelled.

With guards' hands pushing him forward, Omar turned around and gazed at us. I could see the worry in his eyes. He looked like a kid who had just been arrested.

The guards opened a door and led the Ovozis into a room. When Kevin and I reached the door, it was slammed shut in our faces.

"I can't believe this is happening," I told Kevin.

We leaned back against the wall and slunk to the floor. Kevin performed his most nervous habit: rubbing his tooth with his finger until it made a squeaky noise.

Meanwhile, on a TV monitor next to the Connie's Pizza stand, we watched a nightmare play out before our eyes.

The batter who had hit the two-out foul fly ball to Cabrera wound up cracking a double. Both runners scored, tying the game. He himself scored on a single, making it 5–4. And now, in the bottom of the ninth with the game on the line, the Cubs went down, one-two-three. Omar's cup of Pepsi was the reason they lost the game.

When the final out was made, the crowd vented its anger with a chorus of "boos." As they left their seats and flooded into the concourse area, many fans were visibly upset.

"Why do these things always happen to us?" pouted a redheaded young woman in a Cubs cap.

"It was that kid who blew the game," barked a grumpy old man. "Just when things start to look up, something like this happens."

"I feel so sorry for that boy," a mother told her two young sons. "That's all Chicago is going to talk about."

As we watched the fans rumble by and grumble about our friend, I felt sick to my stomach. Sure, Omar was weird, but he wasn't a bad kid.

"Well, at least it was just one game," I managed to say. "They're still in first place."

"It's not like they could blow a five-game lead with ten games to go," Kevin said.

A man in a mustache and a "1908" T-shirt overheard Kevin.

"What did you say?" the man asked.

"Huh?" Kevin replied. "I just said that they're still five games ahead of the Reds, so that should be safe."

"Son, you're so naïve," the man said with a chuckle. "This is the Cubs we're talking about!"

Kevin noticeably gulped. He and I feared the doom that may lie ahead. We didn't want to say it, but we knew what fans would call it.

The Curse of Omar.

Chapter 3

"Mystery Boy Identified"

Along with Mr. Ovozi, my fellow Geeks and I sat in the Cluck 'n' Pluck, a fast-food chicken restaurant in Paw Paw, Michigan. The Cubs had "released" Omar shortly after the Friday game, and we slept that night at his Uncle Sarvar's house in Chicago. On Saturday morning, we decided to just drive home. We stopped in Paw Paw for a quick lunch. With our meals, we all got waters.

No one had the guts to order a Pepsi, or any other soft drink.

Omar sat despondently. Normally, he's happy-go-lucky, rattling off funny one-liners. But during this meal, he couldn't even eat his drumstick. Like Kevin and me, baseball was his life. He understood the profound nature of a baseball curse. We had, after all, grown up with the Indians.

Mr. Ovozi rubbed his son's back.

"You need to eat *something*, Omar," he said.

I remember staring at Omar's glum face. I couldn't imagine what he was going through. He looked back at me.

"What are you staring at me for?" he asked.

"I wasn't . . . ," I mustered.

"Don't stare at me like I'm some sort of freak," he snapped.

A chill ran through me. I don't like to hurt anybody, especially one of my friends.

"Omar!" his dad scolded.

"No, I wasn't thinking . . . ," I stammered.

"Omar, you need to calm down," his dad said. "Joe is your friend. He is on your side. Right, Joe?"

"Yes, of course," I said.

"We're all on your side, dude," Kevin told him.

Omar nodded and buried his face in his hands. Sadly, his troubles were about to get a whole lot worse. Up on the television, a picture of Andres Cabrera appeared on ESPN next to the words "BREAKING NEWS." We turned and watched.

Male news anchor: *Just minutes ago, Major League Baseball announced that Cabrera* *will be suspended for the rest of the regular season, although he will be eligible for the playoffs should the Cubs make it. Though they lead Cincinnati by five games in the NL Central Division, the Cubs will sorely miss Cabrera's big stick. He has carried this offense all year, hitting .332 with 38 homers and 130 RBI.*

At that point, they cut to Omar dropping the Pepsi on Cabrera's head.

Male news anchor: *Chicago fans are pointing the finger of blame on this boy. His slippery fingers not only cost the game for the Cubs, but they also led to Cabrera's suspension and, some fear, another infamous Cubs collapse. For the boy's safety, the team will not reveal his identity. In other baseball news . . .*

The story was so unsettling. If the Cubs kept losing, they would show that clip over and over—and Chicago fans would get angrier and angrier.

"At least they don't know who you are," Kevin told Omar. "Nobody in Chicago knows you except your uncle."

"He won't say anything," Mr. Ovozi said.

"But they know me in Cleveland," Omar said, nervously wringing his hands.

"Yeah, but the video of you is dark," his dad said. "No one can get a good look at your face."

"But," Omar fretted, "there are kids at school who know we went to the game. They'll start telling everyone."

Omar was right. We told everyone at our lunch table that we were going to the Cubs game. Rorie Heffernan, for one, would definitely blab about it.

Omar dropped his head and folded his arms tightly, as if hugging himself. He wouldn't eat another bite of chicken. At this point, none of us were hungry. It was a long drive back to Cleveland, and we had to drive past Detroit to get there.

"Remember that 'Cleveland' video on YouTube?" Kevin asked, trying to cheer Omar up. Kevin started singing the tune on the video:

> *"See a river that catches on fire. . . . We see the sun almost three times a year. . . . It could be worse, though: At least we're not . . . Detroit! We're not Detroit!"*

Normally, Omar would crack up at that. But he didn't even crack a smile. *My gosh,* I said to myself. *This is gonna be a nightmare.*

On Monday morning, Kevin and I arrived at Garfield Heights Middle School. We had to pretend like everything was normal and *hope* that no kids would ask us about the game. While we waited on the blacktop prior to the first bell, we saw Mr. Ovozi's Aztek pulling into a parking space. Omar exited the car with both his mom and dad.

"Crap," Kevin said. "I think they're drawing attention to themselves."

The Ovozis entered the school, obviously to talk to a teacher or the principal. But any hope that Omar's trip to Wrigley would be hushed soon went up in flames.

"Hey, Kernacki!" Rorie Heffernan bellowed to Kevin as he leapt out of his mom's car. A hefty kid with spiked hair, Rorie had a proud-of-myself grin on his face. "Was that Omar who dropped the soda on Cabrera's head?"

Kevin banged his brow and shook his head.

"Can you lower your voice, please?" I told Rorie.

"Lower my voice?" he replied. "Okay."

He then spoke in an exaggeratedly deep voice—but very loudly.

"Was that Omar Ovozi who dropped the Pepsi on Andres Cabrera's head?"

"Shut your stinkin' mouth!" Kevin yelled, but to no avail.

Half the kids on the playground heard Rorie's pronouncement. That was it. The cat was out of the bag. These kids would tell other kids. Before the afternoon was over, it would be all over Twitter—and then all over the Internet.

My mom normally works the 1:00 P.M. to 9:00 P.M. shift at the Vega-Vita health food store. But on Monday, she left early. Like me, my mom is on the smaller side. She has light skin and long, curly brown hair. She has been getting lines around her eyes. I don't know if they're from age or stress.

Mom, my brother Dan, and I live in a wood-framed, lime-green house in the Cleveland suburb of Garfield Heights. My dad lives—temporarily, we hope— two hundred miles away in Dayton, Ohio. That's the only place he could find work. At six o'clock, Mom and I were watching ESPN. C-Pup, my trusty stuffed cocker spaniel, joined us on the couch.

My mom gasped. Flashing across the screen was not just the familiar video of Omar dropping the Pepsi, but the following words: "Mystery boy identified as Omar Ovozi of Garfield Heights, Ohio." My mom jumped to her feet, irate.

"Why are they broadcasting his name?"

"It doesn't matter," I said. "The whole nation knows already."

Even my brother, who wandered into the living room, seemed troubled. Normally, Dan, who was fourteen, was only interested in his electric guitar and heavy metal. But now he stood there, in his fuzzy goatee and Iron Maiden T-shirt, with a rare look of concern.

"Is Omar going to have to flee the country?" he asked.

"No, Danny," Mom said with a sigh.

"Maybe he has family in Uzbekistan," he said.

Mom turned off the TV and sat back on the couch, looking helpless.

"I can't believe this," she said. "Last weekend, he and Kevin slept over our house. I made you guys the sugar cookies that looked like baseballs. Remember? With the red icing for the stitches?"

I nodded.

"Now," Dan quipped, "the *last* thing Omar wants to see is a baseball. Right, Super Joe?"

"Shut up!" I snapped.

"Joey!" Mom scolded.

"He's always trying to get me aggravated!" I said. "Even in a moment like this."

Dan laughed to himself. Maybe it was nervous laughter . . . or maybe he was just a jerk.

"Danny, just go to your room right now, please," Mom said.

"Fine," he replied as he left. "All my stuff's in there."

"Come on, Joey," Mom said to me while grabbing her purse. "Let's see what's going on."

Mom and I walked the two blocks to the Ovozis' home. Omar lived in a simple red-brick ranch house on a street thick with maple trees. On this cloudy, windy day, the leaves rustled loudly. It was usually a pleasant, peaceful street, but not on this day. A swarm of news trucks and more than a dozen reporters had set up in front of the Ovozis' house. Police set up barricades, preventing cars from driving by.

"This is so wrong," Mom said.

My mom took my hand and walked right past the barricades, toward the front door. She told the officer on the porch that we were friends, and Mrs. Ovozi invited us in. Omar's mom is a tall, slender African-American woman with long cornrows. Her mascara was smudged under her cheeks. She obviously had been crying. My mom gave her a long hug.

What I most remember is Mr. Ovozi yelling at a young police officer who sat at the dining room table.

"What are we supposed to do?!" Mr. Ovozi shouted. "Live like this for the rest of our lives?"

"No, sir," the officer replied.

"All these trucks, these media, these paparazzi, get 'em off our street! Right now—just get 'em out of here!"

"Sir, if you would just listen, I've tried to tell you about the laws for freedom of the press, and how—"

"Freedom of the press! What about *my* freedom? Huh? When I grew up, Uzbekistan was part of the Soviet Union. Communist. I came to United States so I could have my freedom. And now you tell me that in the USA—in 'land of the free'—we have to be prisoners in our own house? And for what? Because my son drops his soda at a baseball game?"

Amid the rant, I asked Mrs. Ovozi if I could see Omar. She thought that was a good idea, so I went to his room. I was a little nervous. His door was open, and I popped my head in. I'll never forget what I saw.

Omar's room had always been filled with baseball stuff. He once had posters on the wall of Indians mascot Chief Wahoo and the 1948 Indians, the last Cleveland team to win a World Series. But those posters had been torn down. All of his baseball stuff had vanished. His Grady Sizemore bobblehead, his Baltimore Orioles desk lamp, his cap collection of nearly every American League team, which once lined his shelves—all gone.

Omar sat curled up on the floor, against the wall, between his bed and dresser. He lifted up his head and revealed a devastated expression. His eyes were red. His cheeks glistened with tears.

"Hey," I said.

He nodded. I walked in slowly and sat on the bed. I had no idea what to say. But Omar had been my friend since kindergarten. He was the first kid to ever hang around with me at recess. We had played on the same Little League team every summer. When I cried after striking out to end a game, he put his arm around me and said we should go out for ice cream. Omar was a stand-up guy. A true friend. It felt right just to be there with him.

"What's going to happen to me, Joe?" he asked softly.

"What do you mean?" I said.

"With Bartman, the TV trucks surrounded his house just like mine," he said. "And he got death threats. He had to leave the state."

"Well, this is different," I said. "A, you've already left Illinois. B, you're a kid; nobody's gonna send death threats to a kid. And C, the Bartman thing knocked the Cubs out of the playoffs. This year—I mean, even without Cabrera—the Cubs are going to hang on and make it."

Omar looked in my eyes and shook his head.

"Look at the phone, Joe," Omar said. On the dresser lay his dad's iPhone. "Look at it."

I picked it up. Omar had been following the current Cubs game. I saw the score.

"It's still 8–0 Pittsburgh, isn't it?" he said.

I shook my head.

"No, it's, uh . . . 8–1. . . . Final."

The Cubs' lead over the Reds had shrunk to four games. Omar buried his head and clutched his body. He started to tremble. Then he started to shake. I didn't know what to do.

"Can you get my mom?" he asked, weakly.

"Yeah," I said.

The next afternoon, Kevin and I hung out in his backyard. It was a tiny yard, with a vegetable garden and a chain-link fence. His grandma owned the little white-brick house, and Kevin and his dad lived with her.

Kevin and I had tried to play catch, but we soon lost interest. We plopped on the lawn and fiddled with grass and twigs.

"You should have seen him, Kev," I said. "He looked like he should be in a mental hospital."

Kevin shook his head.

"I was looking at the Cubs' Facebook page," he said. "They're all about the Curse of Omar. And if the Cubs keep losing, it's gonna get a whole lot worse."

We were silent for a long time. But as I sat there, wondering what we could do for our friend, it dawned on me. My phone. I had taken a photo during the fly ball. I pulled the phone out of my pocket and flipped it open. It's a crummy flip phone, and it takes grainy pictures. But when I looked at the photograph, for the very first time, I was startled by what I saw on the screen.

"What is it?" Kevin asked.

Squinting at the small image on the phone, I could see the fans crowded together. They were looking up at the fly ball that was coming toward them. But sneaking up behind the fans was one of those obnoxious Reds fans—the one with the Joey Votto jersey. He had left his seat but not the ballpark.

"That's one of those dudes who was sitting behind us!" Kevin said.

"Yeah," I said, "and look what he's doing."

Kevin peered at the photo. The Votto guy was crouched low, so he wouldn't be noticed, and his hand was on Omar's drink.

"Omar didn't *drop* his Pepsi," I said. "This guy pushed it out of his hand—on purpose!"

"What a jerk!" Kevin cried.

"He *knew* it would make Cabrera drop the ball," I said.

"And then he ran away and made Omar—an eleven-year-old kid—take the fall for it!" Kevin said.

We were both angry yet excited. This was photographic evidence that could clear our friend's name.

"Let's go!" Kevin said, and we ran to our bikes. We couldn't wait to tell Omar the big news.

Chapter 4

THE SEARCH FOR BLAKE UTLEY

Kevin and I sped the four blocks to Omar's house, expecting to see the "media circus." But all the TV trucks were gone. Mr. Ovozi's Pontiac Aztek wasn't even in the driveway. We rode up to a police car, where a young, clean-cut officer sat sleepily in the driver's seat.

"What's up, guys?" he said.

Kevin, whose heart was racing, took the lead.

"We're here to see Omar," he said.

"Sorry," the officer replied. "The family left this morning.".

"Where'd they go?" I asked.

"Can't tell ya," he said. "They're trying to find some privacy."

Kevin bit his lip, trying to think of the next step.

"Joe, show him your picture," he said.

I opened the photo on the phone and handed it to the officer. We explained everything to him, but he wasn't impressed.

"This could be any game," he said, handing the phone back to me. "And it's so small and grainy, you can't make out anything."

We argued our point for a while, but the officer couldn't have cared less. We rode off on our bikes before Kevin pulled to a stop.

"We've got to go to the press with this," he said.

"What do you mean, the press?" I asked. "The *Cleveland Plain Dealer*?"

That newspaper was downtown. We couldn't get there on our bikes. But the Garfield Heights paper was within biking distance, at a local strip mall. That's where we headed.

"We're looking for the sports editor," Kevin said as we walked into the one-room storefront. A burly man with long, white sideburns got up from his desk.

"I'm the news editor, sports editor, lifestyle editor—all in one," he chuckled. "What can I do for you?"

We showed him the photo on the phone. We thought it was the story of the year, but he wouldn't run it.

"I'm not saying you're not friends with that Omar kid," he said. "But you can't see his face in this photo. All I see is a bunch of bodies from the rear. This could be any game, any place, any time."

Kevin and I were frustrated, but we were determined to prove the innocence of Omar—wherever he was. On Wednesday, for the third straight day, he failed to show up for school. Mrs. Reddick, our teacher, said he was doing his work from home, even though he wasn't at *home* home.

Meanwhile, the curse was getting worse. With a loss that afternoon at St. Louis, the Cubs saw their lead shrivel to 3 ½ games. With Cabrera out of the lineup, the Cubs were struggling to put runs on the board. On ESPN's *Pardon the Interruption*, Omar was the source of a heated debate.

Host 1: *They're calling this the Curse of Omar. Is that fair or no?*

Host 2: *First of all, it has not yet reached curse status. If they fail to win the division, it will become a curse.*

Host 1: *The Curse of Omar?*

Host 2: *Hey, I don't want to throw this kid under the bus.*

Host 1: *Ten seconds. Curse of Omar—yes or no?*

Host 2: *If the Cubs don't make the playoffs, it will definitely be because of the Pepsi incident. So, yeah, then you'll have your Curse of Omar—if that's what you want to call it.*

That evening, Kevin and I gathered for a pow-wow in my bedroom. He sat on the bed with my stuffed dog, C-Pup, and petted him nervously.

"We've got to identify this guy," Kevin said about the Reds fan in the photo.

"That's impossible," I said.

"Maybe not," he said. "We know they were from the Cincinnati area. What were they talking about when they were sitting behind us?"

"They were just ripping into the Cubs," I replied.

"No, they were talking about other stuff," Kev said.

Kevin usually only got average grades because he didn't study much. But my mom said he was one of the sharper knives in the drawer. If anyone could piece this case together, he could.

"I remember them talking about a cafeteria," he said. "I remember some of the names they mentioned. Like Barry Larkin."

"He used to play for the Reds," I said. "That's not really a clue."

"All right. But there were others," Kev said. "Daniel Hall. They said his name a lot. And something about Dino or Dino's. And there was that other guy—Ronnie Woo, or something. What else?"

I grabbed a notebook and jotted down every name or topic of conversation we could think of. We came up with a few, and then we looked them up on my mom's laptop.

Ronnie Woo Woo turned out to be a famous Cubs fan. He often said "wooooo" at the end of his cheers. The Reds guys were probably dissing him. Anyway, that didn't help.

But Dino's and Daniel Hall? Bingo! We Googled "Dino's and Cincinnati" and came up with Papa Dino's. That's a pizza place on the campus of the University of Cincinnati. We knew the guys were college age, so that's probably where they went to school. As for

Daniel Hall, it wasn't a guy but instead a dormitory.

"Daniels Hall!" Kevin exclaimed when it popped up in our Google search. "That's it! That's got to be where they live!"

It was a brilliant deduction, but Kevin and I couldn't ID these guys from our computer in Cleveland. Nothing online provided the pictures or even the names of the Daniels Hall residents.

"There's only one thing to do," Kevin insisted. "Drive to Daniels Hall and look for these guys."

"Yeah, but one problem," I said. "Cincinnati is five hours away . . . and we don't drive!"

Neither my mom nor Kevin's father was on board with this plan. Omar's cell phone number had been changed, and we couldn't reach him or his family. But one guy stepped to the plate: my dad.

He's an airplane mechanic, and he lost his job in Cleveland more than a year earlier. He found work three hours away in Dayton, and we've seen him only about once or twice a month. But Dad had been bothered by the Omar events, too. When I asked him if he could come home this weekend and drive us to Cincinnati, he agreed.

My dad is kinda short, like me, but he's tough and hardworking. He played linebacker in high school, and he spent four years in the National Guard. He believes in clean living. He has no tattoos, piercings, or facial hair, and he keeps his light brown hair short. He once rented the movie *Do the Right Thing* just because he liked the title.

"Gosh, I hope you follow your dad's example," Mom always says.

Dad said he would come home on Friday evening, and we planned to leave for Cincy early on Saturday morning. In terms of the curse, the tension was building.

The Reds were in Chicago for a three-game series: Friday night, Saturday afternoon, and the season finale on Sunday afternoon. The Cubs' bats had been ice-cold since Cabrera was suspended, and through Thursday they led the Reds in the standings by only two games.

If the Cubs could win just one of the three games against Cincinnati, they'd clinch the division and make the playoffs. The Omar incident would be forgotten. But if the Reds swept all three games, the Cubs wouldn't make the playoffs. The "Curse of Omar" would be cemented into baseball lore.

Kevin and I watched the Friday night game at my house. As I mentioned, when Kevin gets nervous, he rubs his big tooth with his finger, creating a squeaky noise. There was a whole lot of squeaking going on in the bottom of the ninth inning.

The Cubs trailed 2–1, but they loaded the bases with one out. A single could knock in two runs and win the game— and the division.

"Oh, no!" Kevin cried.

The Reds' manager was bringing in their ace reliever: Aroldis Chapman. Known as the "Cuban Missile," Chapman was perhaps the hardest thrower in human history. In 2012, he fired the fastest fastball ever recorded in a major-league game: 105.1 miles per hour! In 71 ⅔ innings that year, he gave up just 35 hits and struck out 122 batters.

"This is the last guy we want to face," I said. "Just a fly ball or grounder would tie the game, but this guy strikes everybody out."

Kevin and I fell to our knees, praying. You could see the worried expressions on the faces in the Wrigley Field crowd. They knew their team was doomed. I was glad, however, to see that at least one person cared for my friend. A middle-aged woman held up a sign that said "Do it for Omar!"

The Cubs batter didn't do it. He didn't crack a game-winning hit. He didn't tie the game with a sacrifice fly or run-scoring grounder. Instead, he struck out on four pitches. The next hitter followed suit. Strike one. Strike two. Strike three. Game over.

"Darn it!" Kevin yelled, pounding the floor.

The Cubs now led the Reds by just one game with two games to go.

"You know," Kevin said, "these Cubs are going to go up in flames, and I'm not gonna let Omar take the fall!"

"I like your spirit," said a man's voice.

I turned around, and there was my dad. He had just walked in the front door. I stood up, and he gave me a long hug.

"Do you think you two can identify that Reds fan if you see him?" Dad asked.

"I'm pretty sure," Kevin said.

"All right, then let's give it a try," Dad said. "You and Omar are like nephews to me, and I'm tired of him taking the blame for this."

We were all pumped to get to Cincinnati and Daniels Hall.

"Can we leave right now?" I asked.

"We'll leave at six in the morning," Dad said. "Be ready."

And we were. At the crack of dawn, Kevin was standing in our driveway in his Indians jacket. He was admiring my dad's car, which wasn't really my dad's.

"Cool ride!" Kevin said of the deep-red Dodge Challenger. A Challenger is a sporty "muscle" car, like a Ford Mustang or Chevrolet Camaro.

"Thanks," Dad said as we climbed in. "It belongs to my boss. I told him we were on a mission to save Omar, and he handed me his keys. He said, 'This will get you there a little bit faster.'"

The Challenger's engine growled as Dad merged onto the highway. Kevin's face was beaming.

"How fast does this go?" I asked, proudly.

"I won't be speeding, Joe," Dad said.

"I know, but how fast?" I asked

"A hundred and seventy," he replied.

"Sweet!" Kevin exclaimed.

Four hours later, we roared into Cincinnati. Spotting Daniels Hall on the U of C campus was easy. It was a towering presence—a red-brick building twelve stories high.

Our task was daunting: find at least one of the two Reds fans amid the (gulp) seven hundred students who lived in the building.

The big problem was that Kevin and I didn't exactly remember what the two guys looked like. We knew they were white and athletic and had short hair, and we vaguely recalled their faces.

As we roamed the lobby, cafeteria, and dorm-room hallways, we saw about twenty guys who looked like that.

Fortunately, Kevin had a plan, which earned my dad's approval. With a notebook and pen, Kev and I walked up to a guy who looked like our potential Reds fan.

"Excuse me," I said.

"Yes?" he replied.

"We're doing a class project to see how much today's young people know about our national pastime," I said. "So we were wondering if you wouldn't mind taking our baseball trivia challenge."

"Hah!" he said. "Sorry, guys, but I don't follow baseball."

That was fine. We crossed him off our suspect list. A minute later, Kevin spotted a potential candidate—a guy in a U of C Bearcats hoody who was getting off the elevator.

"I think this might be the guy who was in the Votto jersey," Kev said.

The guy, who introduced himself as Brian, accepted our trivia challenge.

"When was the last year the Cubs won the World Series?" I asked.

"Uhm . . . like two hundred years ago—I don't know," he said.

"Who is Ronnie Woo Woo?" Kevin asked.

"Ronnie who-who?" he responded.

"Sorry," Kevin said, "but you failed the test."

"I failed the . . . . What kind of test is this?"

"To be honest," I said, "we're trying to find two Reds fans who were at Wrigley Field last Friday."

"That game where the kid spilled the pop?" Brian asked.

"Yeah, he's our friend," Kevin said.

"That Omar kid is your friend?" Brian asked.

"Our best friend," I said. "We think a Reds fan who lives here knocked the cup out of his hand."

Brian's eyes widened. He headed toward a quiet corner of the lobby.

"Come over here," he said, waving his hand.

We headed over. My dad, who had been monitoring us from afar, joined us.

"I know the person you're talking about," Brian said in a hushed voice. "He was bragging about it last Saturday in the cafeteria. He said if the Reds make the playoffs, the team should pay him a million bucks, because he's the guy who knocked the Pepsi out of that kid's hand."

"You're serious," my Dad implored.

"Oh, yeah," he said. "But then when it was all over the news, he got quiet. He doesn't want to get in trouble."

I showed Brian the photo on my phone.

"Yeah, that looks like him," Brian said.

"What's his name?" my dad asked.

Brian was hesitant to respond. My dad, though, wasn't going to leave without an answer.

"Look, son," my dad implored him. "This guy is ruining the life of an eleven-year-old boy, and now he's hiding like a coward. If he's not going to take responsibility, we need to *make* him take responsibility. Do you hear what I'm saying?"

Brian nodded.

"His name is Blake Utley," Brian said. "He lives on my floor, but he's not here now. He and some of the big Reds fans went back to Wrigley for the final series."

My dad shook Brian's hand, and Kevin and I exchanged excited glances. We had learned the guy's name! The question now was, how would we get ahold of him? We asked students in the dorm, but no one knew his cell phone number.

Kevin started to panic again.

"We've got to find this Utley guy by tomorrow," Kevin said. "If the Cubs blow the division, fans are gonna come down on Omar like an atomic bomb."

As we lunched at Papa Dino's, our fears began to morph into reality. Fans in the restaurant cheered as they watched the Reds tee off on Cubs pitching. After two innings, it was 9–0 Reds. This game was all but over, meaning the Cubs and Reds would be tied for first place. Their Sunday afternoon match-up would decide the division winner.

"There's only one thing we can do," my dad said. "Go to Wrigley Field for Sunday's game—and find Blake Utley."

Chapter 5

SAVING OMAR

~~~~~~~~~~~~~~~~~~~~~~~~~~~~

A chill was in the air. When we arrived at Wrigley Field at noon on Sunday—after spending the night at a Motel 6—it felt much different than our previous visit. The last time, it was a sunny, summery day. Fans had a skip in their step and wore happy-day expressions.

Now, cool October winds blew through the Windy City. The sky was overcast, and so were the faces. Fans, many dressed in their Cubs jackets and wool hats, looked serious, worried. They understood the magnitude of the game.

Two middle-aged men discussed the matter while buying peanuts outside the ballpark.

"If I were a normal fan," the one guy said, "I'd be like, 'Hey, we got a chance to make the playoffs!' But all I can think about is that we're about to witness another Cubs collapse."

As fans descended on the ballpark, we could read their minds. Omar, they were undoubtedly thinking. *That darn kid Omar. We wish he never existed.*

My dad led Kevin and me to Wrigley Field's main gate. We did not have tickets, but my dad had scored an appointment with the head of Wrigley security.

Soon, we were sitting in an old, cramped office deep inside the ballpark. Bob Murphy, a round-shouldered man with a bushy mustache, introduced himself. As Kev would say later, "He looked like one of those 'Da Bears' guys." To my surprise, he tried to help us.

First of all, Bob actually confirmed that Blake Utley had attended the Friday night "Omar game."

"Yep, there's his name," Bob said, showing us his computer screen. "We mailed tickets to the residence of Blake Utley on September 5 for the September 22 game."

"It says Section 102, Row 21, Seats 1 and 2," Dad said, looking at the screen. "Where is that?"

Bob handed us a color-coded seating chart and pointed to the seats. It was right where Kevin and I had sat.

"But what about this game?" I asked. "Where is he sitting?"

Bob looked up Utley on the computer but came up empty. This time, Utley hadn't bought tickets from the Cubs online.

"Either a friend ordered the tickets or they got them from someone else," Bob said. "Or he's simply not here."

"No," my dad said, "he's gotta be here."

"Look," Bob said to my dad. "We'd love to help. Nobody in the Cubs organization—from the owner to the manager to the players—wants Omar to take the heat. But that cell phone photo only shows Utley's backside. We don't know what the guy looks like."

"But *we* do," I said, pointing to Kevin.

"Then it's time to play detective," Bob said, addressing Kevin and me.

He handed all three of us ballpark ID cards to wear around our necks—as well as walkie-talkies.

"You're on a mission," Bob said. "March around the ballpark, from the home plate seats to the center-field bleachers. If you find Blake Utley, hit that red button. We'll send a security team ASAP."

"We can do that," I said.

"Good!" Bob said. "I want to find this guy—and get him to confess—before this game ends. And if we do, I'll let the media know immediately."

"Yes, sir!" Kevin said.

And with that, we began our mission. Kev and I zipped up our Indians jackets and pulled on our wool hats. Together with my dad, we dashed out to the concourse area.

"When I last saw Omar," I told my dad, "the Cubs were four games up and he was devastated. If the Cubs lose this game and the curse becomes real . . . I mean . . . he's gonna be. . ."

"I know, Joe," Dad said. "We got to find this guy."

It was 1:20, a few minutes before game time. Many in the sold-out crowd had settled into their seats, but thousands more were still pouring in. As an opera singer sang the National Anthem, we returned to the "scene of the crime": the left-field seats. We tried to move quickly, but it was hard to maneuver through the heavy crowd.

"You've got to be Walter Payton to walk around here," my dad said, referring to the great Chicago Bears running back.

Eventually, we reached Section 102.

"Do you see him?" my dad asked.

Kev and I walked to the front row and looked upward.

"Man, it's just a sea of faces," I said, worried that we might not find our POI. (That's detective talk for "person of interest.")

"Look for the red," Kevin said.

We saw Reds fans in Section 102, but none of them were Blake Utley.

"You're sure he's not here?" Dad asked.

"Pretty sure," I replied.

"I remember the aggravating smirk on his face," Kevin said. "When I see it again, I'll know."

We moved on, circling the ballpark. Our passes allowed us to go anywhere. After we navigated the lower level, we walked up the long ramps to the upper deck. It was freezing up there, with strong winds whipping in off Lake Michigan. We toured the upper level, looking and looking. . . .

Baseball fans come in all varieties, I was thinking. I saw three nuns huddled together under a blanket. A wide-eyed Latino boy wore his baseball glove, optimistically thinking he would catch a foul ball. We even saw a couple of boys our age, holding up a sign. "Win It for Omar," it said. Kevin appreciated the support. "Thank you," he cried out to them.

We circled the lower and upper levels once each, with no sign of Blake Utley. Meanwhile, Joey Votto smashed a two-run homer, putting the Reds up 2–0.

"The way the Cubs have been hitting," a peanut vendor told a fan, "those two runs may be all the Reds need."

Kevin started rubbing his tooth—a sure sign that he was getting worried. If the Cubs lost this game, the "Curse of Omar" would be all over the TV news. People in Europe, Asia, even Uzbekistan—watching on CNN—would see our pal's face on television, with the word "Curse" underneath it. My dad could see the frustration and stress on my face.

"Are you okay, Joe?" he asked.

"What if we don't find this guy?" I replied. "Today or ever? What if Brian got everything wrong, or what if Utley denies being involved?"

"I'm afraid Omar's gonna go into hiding forever, like Steve Bartman," Kevin said. "I'm afraid we'll never see him again."

Our concerns made my Dad even more determined.

"Let's keeping searching," Dad said. "Let's get this guy."

We continued looking, marching at a faster pace. The task seemed impossible;

more than forty thousand fans were packed inside. Meanwhile, we were almost out of time. With Josh Hamlin on the mound—the Cubs' fastest-working pitcher—the game was speeding along. It entered the sixth inning, still 2–0.

Kevin and I needed to take a bathroom break, which at Wrigley Field is never a pleasant experience. Instead of urinals, the men's rooms have long, metal troughs that you pee into. I peed into one side of a trough, Kevin peed into the other side, and a guy wedged in between us.

Now, normally when you go pee in a men's room, you keep your head down. You focus on the task at hand and avoid making eye contact with strangers. But Kevin and I were in a different mindset that day. I peeked up at the guy between us. Kevin did the same. *Oh my gosh, I* thought. I leaned forward and looked at Kevin, who was equally shocked. Peeing between us was—without a doubt—Blake Utley!

Kevin was too panicked to talk. But somehow, I was able to utter the words.

"Are you . . . ," I said to Utley, "the guy who knocked the pop out of Omar's hand?"

Utley's eyes grew big and his jaw dropped. He was shocked that some kid would know his secret. Yet for a strong moment, I could read the look of guilt on his face.

Utley didn't answer me. He zipped up his zipper, buttoned the top of his jeans, and headed toward the exit.

I can't speak for Kevin, but I had never used a men's room without washing my hands. On this day, I made an exception. When Utley saw that we were following him, he sprinted out the door. We ran after him. My dad, who was waiting outside the men's room for us, caught my eye.

"That's him!" I shouted to Dad. "Blake Utley!"

My dad morphed into linebacker mode, pursuing the POI. Utley was fast, but he struggled to slither through the crowded concourse. Dad, Kevin, and I remained hot on his tail. All the while, Dad was calling security on his walkie-talkie.

"We're after him!" Dad blared. "Section 115!"

Utley busted through the Connie's Pizza line, causing yet another kid to spill his pop. We kept after him. Then, out of the blue, three security guards—including Bob Murphy—jumped in front of his path.

Utley slammed on the brakes and ran back our way. He thought he could plow through us two kids and my old man, but boy was he wrong!

My dad charged into him like an All-Pro defender greeting a ballcarrier, and Kevin and I piled on. Together, we brought him to the ground. My dad held him down until the security guards took over.

"Are you Blake Utley?" Bob asked.

"Yes," Utley said as the guards pulled him to his feet.

"You're coming with us," Bob said. "And you have a whole lot of explaining to do."

As Bob and his men took Utley away, the three of us followed.

"Are you kids okay?" Dad asked us.

We were fine, but Dad looked a bit shaken up.

"That was my first tackle in twenty-five years!" he said proudly.

Utley had gone down in the top of the seventh inning. By the eighth, "breaking news" spread like wildfire. Dad, Kevin, and I huddled in front of a TV near the Connie's Pizza booth. The Cubs game was on ESPN, and these words scrolled below:

> *The Cubs have announced that eleven-year-old Omar Ovozi was NOT responsible for spilling Pepsi on Andres Cabrera during the September 22 Cubs–Reds game.*

"Oh, my gosh!" I cried, excitedly.

"Yes!" Kevin shouted, pumping his fist.

We read on:

> *Reds fan Blake Utley, age twenty, has admitted to knocking the cup out of the boy's hand. Utley said he intentionally tried to*

spill soda on Cabrera's face so that he would not catch the ball.

"Yeahhhhh!" Kev and I blared, jumping up and down and smacking each other with double high-fives.

"I hope Omar is watching this," Dad said.

"If he is," Kevin said, "he's probably like this."

Imitating Omar, Kevin stretched out his arms, wiggled his fingers, and busted out a couple karate moves.

"That's so Omar!" I said, cracking up.

Meanwhile, more good news was brewing. With two men on in the eighth, Cubs' slugger Manny Costada rocketed a shot into left field. We ran toward the seats to witness the historic blast. Amid a deafening roar, the ball sailed out of Wrigley and onto Waveland Avenue.

The Cubs were up 3–2! Fans from two to ninety-two jumped up and down, pumping their fists in the air. Kevin gave me a big "guy" hug, and Dad emitted a loud "woooo-hoooo!"

Should the Cubs win, anything associated with the "Curse of Omar" would be completely forgotten. Happy days would return to Wrigleyville.

And the Cubs *did* win. Chicago closer Bobby "Lights Out" Lackey struck out the side in the ninth. And what a scene! Cubs players mobbed their pitcher. Delirious fans—believing that this could be the year—sang the Wrigley victory song "Go, Cubs, Go!"

Outside the park, thousands of fans from nearby neighborhoods poured into the streets.

"We'll never be able to get out of Chicago!" my dad shouted amid the noise.

As it turned out, we didn't need to. The National League Division Series would start on Wednesday, and the Cubs invited us to attend Game 1. In fact, they treated us like heroes. They paid for Dad, Kevin, and me to stay in the world-famous Drake Hotel. They got ahold of the Ovozis and flew them in for the game.

We were in the Drake's lobby when Omar and his parents arrived. Omar walked through the front door wearing a Cubs cap. When he saw us, he threw his arms up in the air and broke into a huge smile.

"Dudes!" he shouted

We ran up to him, slapping high-fives.

"Man, I don't know how to thank you guys," Omar said.

"Eh, it was nothin'," I said, as my dad rolled his eyes.

"So what happened to you?" Kevin asked. "Did they throw you in the nut house?"

They didn't throw him in the nut house, Omar explained. But he did have to undergo psychological counseling. The "cure" was Blake Utley's admission of guilt—coupled with the Cubs' victory.

Omar was sky-high prior to Game 1. The Cubs let him throw out the ceremonial first pitch. Amid chants of "O-Mar! O-Mar! O-Mar," our fellow Baseball Geek fired a perfect strike to the catcher. Omar threw his hands in the air as if he had just won the World Series.

Fans waved signs, including "Chicago Loves the Cleveland Kids!"

Afterward, we took our seats behind the left-field fence. And in the seventh inning, guess who got to sing "Take Me Out to the Ball Game?" Bob Murphy led us to the WGN broadcast booth to lead the crowd in that familiar song. I was scared and just kind of mumbled the lyrics in the background. But Kevin and Omar are a couple of hams. Like Harry Caray of old, they leaned out of the booth, swayed back and forth, and boomed the words into their microphones.

It's root, root, root for the
Cub-bies, (we didn't dare say Indians!)
If they don't win it's a shame,
For it's one! Two! Three strikes you're out
At the ollllld balllll gaaaame!

And then Omar added the tack-on line that Harry used to say: "Let's get some runs!"

The fans went crazy, and many of them stared up at us and beamed big smiles. The three of us were elated.

"You deserve this," Kev said to Omar, "after all you've been through."

To top it off, the Cubs were routing the Phillies 6–2 thanks to four RBI from Andres Cabrera. We returned to our left-field seats, where we planned to enjoy the rest of the game.

But for some reason, the baseball gods can never just leave us alone.

In the top of the ninth, Phillies slugger Ryan Howard blasted a towering fly ball to left. It sailed over the fence for a home run, bounced high off a concrete step, and landed right in Kevin's hands.

"Throw it back!" the fans chanted. "Throw it back!"

"What are they saying?" my dad asked.

"It's a Cubs tradition," I told him. "When an opposing player hits a home run, the fans are supposed to throw it back onto the field. It's kinda like, 'We don't want your stinkin' home run.'"

Not wanting to disappoint the fans, Kev reared back and chucked the ball onto the field.

There was only one problem. Left fielder Cabrera had his back turned to us, and Kevin's throw hit him right in the noggin! The Cubs' superstar dropped to the ground like a sack of potatoes!

The crowd gasped, and then went stone-silent. All eyes turned to Cabrera, who was kneeling on the grass with his head down, and then to Kevin, whose expression said "uh-oh. . . ." Finally, after a moment that seemed like an eternity, Cabrera jumped to his feet and waved his cap to the crowd. He was all right, and the fans burst into applause.

My fellow Geeks and I plopped in our chairs, emitting a collective "phew!"

"Remind me," Omar said, "never to come back to Wrigley Field."

Read each title in The Baseball Geeks Adventures

A HALL Lot of Trouble at Cooperstown
The Baseball Geeks Adventures Book 1

When Joe, Kevin, and Omar take a trip to Cooperstown to save Kevin's dad, will the boys be able save themselves from the "trouble" they get into?

ISBN: 978-1-62285-118-8

Foul Ball Frame-up at Wrigley Field
The Baseball Geeks Adventures Book 2

After Omar is "framed" for an incident that was out of his hands, can Joe and Kevin save their friend from becoming one of the biggest curses in history?

ISBN: 978-1-62285-123-2

The Treasure Hunt Stunt at Fenway Park
The Baseball Geeks Adventures Book 3

Joe, Kevin, and Omar want a shot at the Treasure Hunt Round. But can the Geeks beat the Little League Champs before they "stunt" the Geeks' chances of winning it all?

ISBN: 978-1-62285-128-7

Bossing the Bronx Bombers at Yankee Stadium
The Baseball Geeks Adventures Book 4

When the Geeks are invited to watch a game from a luxury suite, Joe, Kevin, and Omar find themselves in a bad situation when they start making some "bossy" calls.

ISBN: 978-1-62285-133-1